Archway Publishing books may be ordered through booksellers or by contacting:

Archway Publishing
1663 Liberty Drive
Bloomington, IN 47403
www.archwaypublishing.com
1 (888) 242-5904

Because of the dynamic nature of the Internet, any web addresses or links contained in this book may have changed since publication and may no longer be valid. The views expressed in this work are solely those of the author and do not necessarily reflect the views of the publisher, and the publisher hereby disclaims any responsibility for them.

Any people depicted in stock imagery provided by Thinkstock are models, and such images are being used for illustrative purposes only. Certain stock imagery © Thinkstock.

ISBN: 978-1-4808-5209-9 (sc)
ISBN: 978-1-4808-5208-2 (hc)
ISBN: 978-1-4808-5210-5 (e)

Print information available on the last page.

Archway Publishing rev. date: 09/15/2017

Dedication........

I want to dedicate this book to all of the wonderful people and friends I know in Moses Lake and Our Lady of Fatima Catholic Church, for just being there.

I also dedicate this book to my grandchildren and all other children who will enjoy reading and listening to it.

.....Acknowledgement..........

First of all, I want to thank Rita Young for saying, after she read the original manuscript, "Why don't you have your book published?", therefore sending me on this journey.

The individual I really want to thank is my partner in life, for 49 years, my lovely wife Joan. She not only put up with me while I put this story together, but also did the original editing.

And I definitely cannot forget all the help I received from Rosalie McDonald. She did all the wonderful editing and encouraging me to bring this story to life.

This brings me to the Children of Fatima Kindergarten who really listened to my story as I read it to them the first time, therefore giving me the spark to "just do it".

Little Crow is hatched in a very tall tree, and when Mama Crow thinks he is old enough, she says "just step up on the ledge of the nest and jump and you can fly". He steps up on the edge of the nest and looks. He finds that jumping is easier said than done. This is the story on how one Little Crow overcomes his fear of the unknown.

Once upon a time a Mama Crow was extremely proud that she finally had a nest, and an egg with her very own little crow inside. She was so happy, that she told her entire family about it.

Uncle Crow just stared at her. Then with a loud "Caw", he flapped his wings and flew over to the next tree. He really couldn't care less. In fact he told her that her baby will be just one more noisy crow to steal his food.

Dad Crow was a little more excited, as he "cawed" really loud as if to say he was proud to be the daddy, but he too flapped his wings and joined Uncle in the next tree.

A couple of weeks went by while Mama Crow sat on her nest keeping the little egg warm while he grew.

Then one day, a miracle happened. A little beak broke through the shell. He struggled to free himself of the stubborn shell, but he just couldn't get out. He pushed, he wiggled and he pecked to get out, but he would get tired, and then quit for awhile.

After two days of watching her young one struggle, Mama Crow finally helped him break the last of the shell that was preventing him from being free. He slept for a long while afterwards as he was totally exhausted from his experience of coming into the world.

When he finally opened his eyes, the first thing he did was a very weak "c-a-w". He was hungry and lonely, because his mother, sensing that he would be hungry, was out finding some food for him. When she came, wow, did he eat. He ate everything she would bring him. And when she wasn't there, he was crying for more. He ate, and ate and ate. So, it wasn't too long before his mother told him it was time for him to learn how to fly........ Do what?

Fly? He hadn't even looked out of the nice warm nest where he was hatched, let alone fly. So, his mother told him, just shut your eyes and jump up on the edge. It's not hard. Then just jump and flap your wings.

When he opened his eyes, he couldn't believe where he was. The nest was suspended in the very tiptop of a huge old Oak tree. He looked over the edge and he just about fainted from the terrible height. In fact, he was so scared that he fell backwards back into the nest knocking himself out on the floor.

Mother Crow came to his aid, and took him in her wings and said nice crow things to him. He was almost as big as she was, but she still mothered him as though he were still little.

Mother Crow then told him that all crows fly. In fact flying is fun, and she took off and soared through the air and dived and then came back to the nest. He looked at her and gave her a look of total disbelief. She wanted him to try ......What?

He would much rather stay cuddled in her wings where it was warm and SAFE! Even though they were high up in the old Oak tree. She talked to him at length convincing him he could do it.

He finally gave in to her coaxing and jumped up on the edge of the nest. He shut his eyes and jumped, flapping his wings like crazy and what happened?

He took a circling leap that went down, down, down and ended up in the tall grass at the bottom of the tree. There he bellowed out a very loud "CAW! CAW! CAW! CAW!" In fact he was so noisy and loud, a couple of squirrels hid from him inside the tree.

He laid there until Mama Crow came down in front of him and told him to try again. She then flapped her wings "cawing" and hopping as if showing him how to do it. Then she would turn around to see if he was following.

The little crow, just looked at her, then waddled over to her and said........ "Caw?". Then she would repeat flapping her wings and hopping away from him. The little crow would, of course copy her again and say "Caw?". Mama Crow and Little Crow did it again and again.

So, Mama Crow finally flew up to the top of another tree to figure out how to help her little one.

Convinced he couldn't fly and afraid of heights, the little crow, who was not so little anymore waddled around trying to find a way back into the nest, which of course was impossible because the nest was in the top of the tree and he was way, way, way down at the bottom of the tree.

All this time, from inside the nearest house the neighbor was watching all of this commotion through the window, and wondered what he could do. The simplest thing, was to ignore the little crow and go about his business. But that is one thing he could not do.

After thinking about the situation, he went into his garage and found an old wooden toy bird with wheels that made a squeaking noise that sounded like the little crow. It also had a long cord attached to it.

So, he cleaned up the old wooden toy bird and he took it out into the yard that night so the unsuspecting little crow would not see him, because the little crow was still sitting in the tall grass.

The next morning, the neighbor started to pull the wooden bird with its squeaking wheels. The little crow, woke up to the noise, and thinking it was his mother, he started to follow it.

The little crow would almost get to it, and the neighbor would pull it ahead. Well, the little crow thought, I will just jump to catch up with mama. But every time he almost made it, the neighbor would pull it again.

So, the little crow jumped and flapped his wings a little bit, because he was getting tired of walking through all that grass. And the neighbor pulled the wooden bird again.

13

Again, the little crow jumped and really did fly until he was over the grass and the neighbor. Little crow was not only surprised at what he had done, that he kept right on really flying into the beautiful blue sky that was his to explore. He circled, he dove, he went upside down and he even flew up to the top of the old Oak tree and the nest where Mama Crow was waiting for him.

She proudly looked at him as if to say I'm proud of you son! Even Papa Crow and Uncle Crow came over to the nest to congratulate Little Crow that he could now fly. Then Little Crow, who was not that little, Mama Crow, Papa Crow and Uncle Crow then flew to the top of the next tree to tell the whole world about the new addition to the family.

This little story tells you, that even though you might be scared when you find yourself out on a limb, that with God's help you too can succeed.

Oh, by the way, this is not the end......
It is just the Beginning.

CPSIA information can be obtained
at www.ICGtesting.com
Printed in the USA
BVOW05s0426101017
497009BV00004B/6/P

9 781480 8520